THIS BOOK
BELONGS TO:

_____

# BIRD
# CHILDREN

# BIRD CHILDREN

## THE LITTLE PLAYMATES OF THE FLOWER CHILDREN

## ELIZABETH GORDON

### ILLUSTRATED BY M. T. ROSS

DERRYDALE BOOKS
NEW YORK

This 2000 edition is published by Derrydale Books™,
an imprint of Random House Value Publishing, Inc.,
280 Park Avenue, New York, New York 10017.

Derrydale Books™ and design are trademarks of
Random House Value Publishing, Inc.

Random House
New York • Toronto • London • Sydney • Auckland
http://www.randomhouse.com/

Printed and bound in Singapore

Cover design by Sandra Wilentz

ISBN 0-517-16362-4

8 7 6 5 4 3 2 1

To all children who love
Birds and Flowers, and
especially to my little friend
Dorothy Virginia,
this book is lovingly dedicated

# FOREWORD

BIRDS are only another expression of God's love, and we are told that not even a sparrow shall fall to the ground without the notice of the Father.

Birds are poetry come to life and set to music. If you have stood at the edge of a forest at sundown and heard the birds singing their good-night songs, heard the sleepy little notes grow fainter and fainter until the silence came,—then when the dusk has deepened, you have heard the night birds begin their plaintive songs, you must realize what a different place our beautiful world would be without birds.

Even in great cities we have always some birds. The saucy little sparrow, who comes so boldly begging crumbs at your window, likes the cities best.

Only very thoughtless people, or those who do not understand, would harm or frighten a bird.

Birds are real little people, and I am sure that when you have come to know them you will love them as much as you have learned to love the flower children.

The publishers and the author have received so many letters from parents commending *Flower Children* for its instructive features, and from children, demanding "more" delightful play-mates, that they offer bird brothers and sisters, believing that "The Little Playmates of the Flower Children" will prove as welcome visitors as "The Little Cousins of the Field and Garden."

The author and the artist wish to thank the children for their many expressions of interest and for their loyal support.

—ELIZABETH GORDON

—M. T. ROSS

#  BIRD CHILDREN

S IR ROOSTER is a noisy chap,
    He wakes you from your morning nap;
    He sleeps but little all night through,
    Crows at eleven, one and two.

9

# BIRD CHILDREN

MRS. HEN, the kind old dame,
 Always dresses just the same;
 She talks all day about her joys,
 And lays nice eggs for girls and boys.

S AID GUINEA HEN: "I like to eat
Three-cornered grains of nice buckwheat;
I only want good, simple food
To feed my fluffy little brood."

DEAR little, downy GOSLING said:
"I can't get learning through my head;
I really don't see what's the use—
When I grow up I'll be a goose."

S AID FATHER GANDER: "I shall take
A stroll this morning to the lake."
MOTHER GOOSE said: "I'll go, too,
And maybe take a swim with you."

13

SAID YELLOW DUCKLING to his brother:
"Come on, let's hide away from mother."
But he replied: "Oh, dear me, no!
We'd better not, she'd worry so."

# BIRD CHILDREN

"**H**ONK-HONK, Honk-honk," old
SNOW GOOSE said,
"I think tonight we'll go to bed
A hundred miles due south from here—
The snow is on the way, I fear."

15

IN shallow water MALLARD DUCK
At fishing sometimes tries his luck;
At other times he thinks it's nice
To nibble at the sweet wild rice.

# BIRD CHILDREN

M ADAM SWAN'S a graceful lady,
Likes to float where banks are shady;
When Father Swan goes out to swim
He takes the cygnets out with him.

17

# BIRD CHILDREN

G OLDEN PHEASANT took a notion
To take a trip across the ocean,
Got a nice room at the zoo
And said he'd stay a year or two.

TAKING his family for a walk
We see old MR. TURKEY COCK;
He dresses up in colors gay—
His wife wears quiet tones of gray.

#  BIRD CHILDREN

OLD DOCTOR STORK, the kind old bird,
Brings the new babies, I have heard;
If you should ask him, he may bring
You one to keep, beneath his wing.

# BIRD CHILDREN

SIR ROOK is English, don't you know?
Says: "Do not confound me with the Crow."
His family tree is large and old,
Which makes his manner proud and cold.

21

# BIRD CHILDREN

P ARADISE BIRD, in her new clothes,
   Said: "They're expensive, goodness knows!
   I s'pose, because they were so dear,
   I'll have to wear them all this year."

*(Red Paradise Bird)*

22

# BIRD CHILDREN

$P$EACOCK'S a bird of much renown
And wears a lovely cap and gown;
They say he's very, very vain
And likes to show his sweeping train.

# BIRD CHILDREN

SAID NIGHTINGALE: "It's not my way
  To practice singing in the day,
    But wait till all the rest are through
    And I will gladly sing for you."

24

#  BIRD CHILDREN

CANARY BIRD said to his mother:
"Is that bird in the tree my brother?"
Mama Canary said: "Oh, no!
He's just a cousin—wild, you know."

ORIOLE, flashing wings of flame,
In the spring like sunshine came,
Hung his nest away up high
So his babes could see the sky.

(*Orchard Oriole*)

#  BIRD CHILDREN

BALTIMORE ORIOLE, pretty thing,
Builds his nest of bits of string;
He 's sociable and likes to stay
Where people live and children play.

27

# BIRD CHILDREN

M EADOW LARK has a flute-like voice,
Sings a song that's very choice;
Builds his nest low, near the ground,
With woven grasses arched around.

# BIRD CHILDREN

**B**LACK, solemn-looking MR. CROW
Steals the good farmer's corn, you know;
If you ask why he breaks the laws,
He answers, wisely: "Caws, caws, caws."

FRIENDLY little CHICKADEE
    Is just as cunning as can be;
    Upon your window-sill he'll come
    And thank you kindly for a crumb.

CARDINAL BIRD wears vivid red,
He 's very amiable, 'tis said;
He likes fresh fruits and seeds to eat
And has a song that 's very sweet.

31

MAGPIE'S a gossip—that's the truth—
A naughty, disobedient youth;
We must not judge him, but suppose
He does the very best he knows.

32

# BIRD CHILDREN

GREAT BLUE HERON likes to fly,
And so he builds his house up high,
'Way in the tops of tallest trees
Where he lives, happy as you please.

# BIRD CHILDREN

**B**OB-O-LINK, among the clover,
Tells his name over and over;
He does n't stay North very long
And when he goes we miss his song.

# BIRD CHILDREN

INDIGO BUNTING comes in May,
Saying cheerfully: "I'm here to stay."
He's a nice, friendly little thing,
Willing at any time to sing.

35

# BIRD CHILDREN

EAGLE has piercing yellow eyes,
He's very strong and very wise;
He's king and master over all
The other birds, both great and small.
*(Golden Eagle)*

# BIRD CHILDREN

TURKEY BUZZARD, on the wing,
Is a most graceful-looking thing;
Like scavengers, who come each day,
He does much good in his own way.

VERMILION FLYCATCHER 's a beauty,
 You 'll always find him right on duty;
Searches for food early and late,
Bringing it to his pink-clothed mate.

# BIRD CHILDREN

Y ELLOW WARBLER comes to stay
Along about the first of May;
He likes to live by pond or rill
And builds his nest with care and skill.

39

CURLEW runs along the shore,
To him, perhaps, it's like a floor;
Whistle, and he will answer you
Something like this: "Kerloo, Kerloo."

*(Long-billed Curlew)*

# BIRD CHILDREN

SIR PARTRIDGE is a drummer bold,
   You'll hear him drum when days are cold.
   He says the nicest things to eat
   Are red thorn apples, ripe and sweet.

*(Ruffed Grouse)*

41

THE SNOWY HERON'S used to be
  A very fine, large family;
  I tell you this with great regret:
  Men hunt the bird their plumes to get.

42

# BIRD CHILDREN

SAID KINGFISHER: "The choicest dish
I know of is a fresh caught fish;
I love to fish, and, if you'll wait,
I'll get you some—I need no bait."

BROWN THRASHER is a cheerful bird,
His sweet, clear carol may be heard
All through the pleasant summer day;
We 're sorry when he goes away.

#  BIRD CHILDREN

SAID GOLDFINCH: "I believe in weeds,
   I live all winter on the seeds;
   In my snug coat of black and gold
   I really do not feel the cold."

# BIRD CHILDREN

CHEER UP, cheer up, it 's going to rain,"
Sang plump SIR ROBIN, "but 't is plain
We need some moisture for the ground,
So dinners may be better found."

# BIRD CHILDREN

F LITTING 'round the swimming pool,
   Where the air is nice and cool,
   RED-WINGED BLACKBIRD sings in glee:
   "Gloogle-ee, Gloogle-ee-e."

47

# BIRD CHILDREN

QUAIL sings a song of sheer delight:
"Bob White, Bob White, Bob-Bob-Bob-White."
I wonder who Bob White may be
To whom he calls so merrily.

# BIRD CHILDREN

K INGBIRD, like some other boys,
Likes to make a lot of noise;
He's a bit boisterous in play
And sometimes quarrelsome, they say.

# BIRD CHILDREN

CATBIRD is good at imitations,
He mimics all his small relations;
And, safely perched upon a bough,
He imitates the cat's "Me-ow."

50

# BIRD CHILDREN

SAID PURPLE MARTIN to his lady:
   "Here's a house all cool and shady;
   I surely am a lucky swallow—
   This beats my building plans all hollow."

51

"CHE-WEE, che-wee, che-wee-che-wee,"
　Said REDSTART, "Will you look at me?
　I do not sing so well by note
　But see my black and orange coat!"

(*American Redstart*)

# BIRD CHILDREN

WITH a flash of bright-hued wing,
BLUEBIRD comes to say it 's spring;
Sets about to build his nest
In the tree which suits him best.

# BIRD CHILDREN

LITTLE SIR SCREECH OWL and his wife
Live such a cheerful, useful life;
They nest among the apple trees,
Saying: "May we eat the bugs here, please?"

 # BIRD CHILDREN

W"HO, WHO, who, who?" asks SIR BARN OWL,
When he comes out at dusk to prowl;
He has great shiny yellow eyes,
And looks so very, *very* wise.

# BIRD CHILDREN

OSTRICH'S cousin, CASSOWARY,
Wears a coat peculiar, very;
It's half like feathers, half like hair—
None other like it anywhere.

#  BIRD CHILDREN

OSTRICH grows to be immense
But he has very little sense,
For when an enemy's at hand
He covers up his head with sand.

# BIRD CHILDREN

SAID PENGUIN, pensively, one day:
"Come, fishie dear, come out and play."
But fishie answered, in a fright:
"I 've heard about your appetite."

# BIRD CHILDREN

ALBATROSS has wings so strong
That he could fly the whole day long;
But if he's tired, he can float
Upon the waves, just like a boat.

#  BIRD CHILDREN

THE dainty MISSES PARRAKEET
Dress all in green and look so sweet;
From South America they came
And Love Bird is their other name.

*(Red-faced Love Birds)*

60

# BIRD CHILDREN

H̲UMMING BIRD, the dainty thing,
 Has no voice and cannot sing,
 He lives daintily, and sips
 Honey from the flowers' lips.

*(Ruby-throated Humming Bird)*

# BIRD CHILDREN

HERE'S a good joke about SPOONBILL:
Never had hair and never will;
His head is absolutely bare,
He's happy though—he does n't care.

*(Roseate Spoonbill)*

# BIRD CHILDREN

M ADAME IBIS, stately bird,
Stands and thinks without a word;
She can't forget that long ago
She was a sort of queen, you know.

*(Scarlet Ibis)*

#  BIRD CHILDREN

SANDPIPER lives beside the water
With her little son and daughter;
Shows the cunning little brood
Exactly where to look for food.

*(Least Sandpiper)*

# BIRD CHILDREN

SAID STORMY PETREL: "This is fine!
I do enjoy the gale called 'line';
No matter how the storm may thicken
It just suits 'Mother Carey's Chicken.'"

65

# BIRD CHILDREN

SAID fussy MADAM COCKATOO:
"I always find enough to do;
I'm such a busy, useful dame,
I know these folks are glad I came."

PARROT'S a very wise old bird,
  She can speak English well, I 've heard;
  Laughs and says in manner jolly:
  "Have you a cracker for Miss Polly?"
  *(Gray Parrot)*

67

A DREADFUL thief is old BLUE JAY,
He robs the other birds, they say;
He wears a handsome suit of blue,
And calls a gay "Good-day" to you.

S PARROW'S an Englishman, I'm told,
   His manners are both rude and bold;
   Other birds wish he'd go away,
   But he says: "No, I've come to stay."

#  BIRD CHILDREN

A T EVENING, when the world is still,
Mournfully sings the WHIP-POOR-WILL;
In his brown suit, all trimmed with white,
He slips softly through the night.

 # BIRD CHILDREN

E AVE SWALLOW, in his nest of clay,
Always has lots of things to say;
He and his brothers often race,
Catching the insects 'round the place.

#  BIRD CHILDREN

SEA-DOVE, sometimes called Little Auk,
  Flies very little, likes to walk;
  He wears a coat of feathers warm,
  And does n't seem to mind the storm.

# BIRD CHILDREN

L OON is a fearless diver bold,
  He does n't mind the heat or cold;
  He dives and swims—oh, very far—
  And then bobs up and laughs, "Ha-Ha!"

# BIRD CHILDREN

$M$OCKING BIRD is very clever,
Uses her own notes hardly ever,
But saucily sings bits of song
Which to the other birds belong.

"O DEAR, dear me!" WOODPECKER said.
"The birds all shout at me, 'Red-head';
It makes me feel so very sad,
No wonder that my temper's bad!"

75

 # BIRD CHILDREN

T O SAVE his little home from harm,
CRESTED FLYCATCHER has a charm:
He finds and places in his nest
A piece of Mr. Snake's old vest.

 # BIRD CHILDREN

I VORY BILLED WOODPECKER said:
"Dear me!
They're cutting down my family tree;
Where can I live, I'd like to know,
If men will spoil the forest so?"

#  BIRD CHILDREN

NIGHTHAWK is lazy, sleeps all day,
And then comes out at night to play;
He always wears his evening clothes
And when it's daylight, home he goes.

#  BIRD CHILDREN

B ARN SWALLOW is a graceful thing,
Catches his food upon the wing;
Perhaps that 's why he is so fond
Of skimming lightly o 'er the pond.

LAUGHING GULL seems free from care,
He 's always laughing everywhere;
He never tells what it 's about
And no one yet has found it out.

# BIRD CHILDREN

STARLING'S a pretty little dear,
  He lives in Europe, too, we hear;
    The folks in Ireland, so we're told,
    Think that he's worth his weight in gold.

  # BIRD CHILDREN

SAID busy little JENNY WREN:
"I like to live where there are men;
I come each year to the same place
So I can see some friendly face."

MOURNING DOVE is very sweet,
   She likes nice grains and seeds to eat;
   In her soft voice she calls: "Coo, coo,"
   Which means in dove-talk, "I love you."

R ED-SHAFTED FLICKER hops around,
Eating the ants upon the ground;
He builds in any hollow tree
Where he's as snug as snug can be.

#  BIRD CHILDREN

G REEN JAY lives in Rio Grande,
    A member of a robber band;
    He 's very beautiful, but, oh,
    We wish he would n't plunder so!

#  BIRD CHILDREN

COWBIRD is lazy, sad to say,
 She lives in quite a selfish way;
 She's neither pretty nor polite
 And never tries to do what's right.

C UCKOO 'S a quiet, useful bird,
   He eats the naughty worms, I 've heard,
   And from the woods he calls to you
   His simple song, "Cuckoo, cuckoo."

# BIRD CHILDREN

THE SNOWBIRD said: "Let's have some fun,
The storm is over—there's the sun."
He rolled and tumbled in the snow,
Like other little ones you know.

*(Snowflake)*

#  BIRD CHILDREN

UNDER a bridge, where all day long
The brooklet sings its happy song,
PHOEBE BIRD builds her nest of clay
To which she comes each year to stay.

SCARLET FLAMINGO said: "Just think!
I really thought this gown was pink,
But when you see it in this light,
It 's red—I fear it 's rather bright."

**H**ERE is old MR. PELICAN,
He is a famous fisherman;
Said he: "I do not mind wet feet
If I catch fish enough to eat."

# BIRD CHILDREN

PUFFIN walks better than he flies,
　　He has red feet and queer white eyes;
　　He is a funny little fellow
　　With his great beak of red and yellow.

*(Sea Parrot)*

# BIRD CHILDREN

L YRE BIRD'S an Australian child,
  She lives in lonely places wild,
  And builds upon the rocky ground
  The queerest nest which can be found.

# INDEX